tough sh*t

Tough Sh*t
Copyright © 2022 by Ken Ng

All rights reserved. No part of this publication may be reproduced, distributed, or transmitted in any form or by any means, including photocopying, recording, or other electronic or mechanical methods, without the prior written permission of the author, except in the case of brief quotations embodied in critical reviews and certain other non-commercial uses permitted by copyright law.

Tellwell Talent
www.tellwell.ca

ISBN
978-0-2288-7456-0 (Hardcover)
978-0-2288-7455-3 (Paperback)

for Dylan, Kora & Jack

a hilarious, relevant project by (jk)

Written by Ken Ng
Illustrated by Jacqueline Monk

Dear Josie,

Some days are going to be awesome, and some are going to suck really, really hard! Always remember that you are Never Alone, your family, And your Auntie Laura will Always be just a phone call away! I will love and support you forever! Make the most of everyday! Appreciate all that you have — and when it gets hard, remember I am here — and tomorrow is a new day!

xoxox
Laura

My # 514-880-6658

I have too much homework

tough sh*t.

We want a dog.

tough sh*t.

My best friend doesn't like me anymore.

tough sh*t.

My brother got more marshmallows than I did.

tough sh*t.

We want to watch more TV.

tough sh*t.

I'm cold but I don't want to wear my jacket.

tough sh*t.

no one will buy me a cell phone.

tough sh*t.

my team didn't win the game.

tough sh*t.

I don't want to have a bath.

tough sh*t.

I didn't eat all my dinner and now I'm hungry.

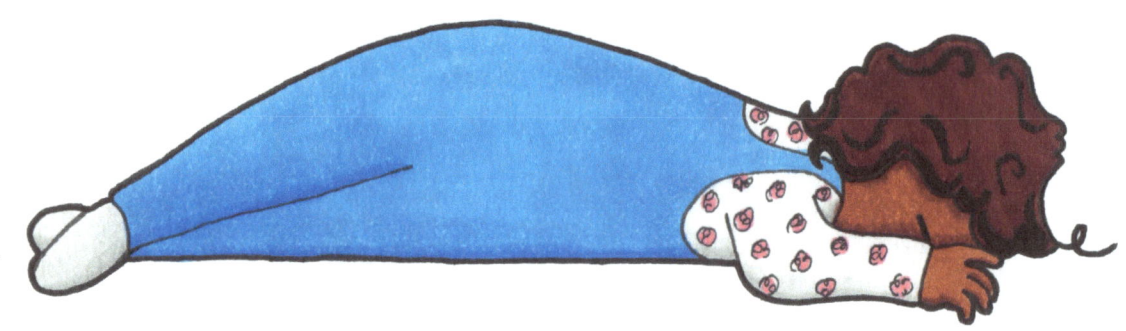

tough sh*t.

Sometimes this world is an unkind place.

Sometimes things won't always go your way.

Sometimes you're not going to get what you want.

And sometimes, you are just going to have to deal with some **<u>tough</u> <u>sh*t</u>**.

but...

I will always, always, **always** be there to love and support you through it all.

No matter what tough sh*t you have to face,

we'll face it together.

CPSIA information can be obtained
at www.ICGtesting.com
Printed in the USA
BVHW022058190322
631912BV00002B/19